Intriguing Ocean

By David G Evans

Table of Contents

The ozone layer was first discovered in 1913 by 2 French physicists Charles Fabry and Henri Buisson. The ozone layer is a region of Earth's massive stratosphere that eminently absorbs the sun's damaging ultraviolet radiation.

From manipulating the weather and the constant spraying of many different chemicals into the atmosphere to stave off global warming only hastened the deterioration of the ozone layer.

The last time that the ozone layer research center sent up there ozone monitoring drone, the atmospheric scientists read over the drones data and said from what they read there was only 2 percent of the ozone layer left.

The next day the scientists met with the president of the United States and conveyed to him there findings.

He was surprised and became very restless; this matter will be dealt with today. This left the scientists scratching their heads, they didn't hear what they wanted to hear.

> “Whom are you going to contact Mr. President?”
>
> “NASA.”

I doubt they're going to be able to deal with such heightened concerns, you should also contact OCFR (Ozone Center for Research).There are 6 layers to Earth’s atmosphere.

If we don't take this seriously then we'll have catastrophic issues with the atmosphere. When we breathe, we're taking in an air mixture of about 78 percent nitrogen, 21 percent oxygen and 1 percent argon, water vapor.

The president developed a concerned look in his weary eyes, I'm wondering how long it's going to take this to be resolved.

"How many days do you think we have left?"

"Judging by our research, 1 month, maybe less."

Chapter 1

Just then the double doors swung open, and several scientists walked in. Written on their lab coats, in blue letters it said Oceanic research. Excuse us Sir, he looked over at them with an authoritative look.

"How did you make it past the Secret Service?"

"We gave them our IDs and told them that we had a meeting with you today."

In an angered voice he said I'll be talking to them after this, I may be firing some of them. What I hate the most is being interrupted, I will not tolerate this next time.

You can all talk now; I'm done with my rant. One of the young men got the courage up to speak, half of the marine life in the Atlantic Ocean is dead.

10% of the Atlantic Ocean, has dried up, all of our coasts are currently being hit by tsunamis. Then the second man spoke, almost every part of Florida is flooded and only getting worse.

There governor called a State of Emergency, and to make the matters worse their grid is completely down. The National Guard is helping the residents to leave to a safer location in Alabama.

In a few days the whole state of Florida will be underwater, military engineers were sent in. They'll be working on making levies and anti-wave barriers, this project will cost 70 million dollars.

Then I'm going to send them relief money, after I'm done listening to you fellas. The ocean drones have recorded a 50 percent upward spike in tsunamis. We have images here from the ocean drones, you'll definitely want to see these images.

The president glared down at the images; I need further explanation on these images. What you are seeing are lightning strikes during the tsunami, even the lightning strikes aren't typical strikes.

The waves are being electricfied, the lightning strikes are blue. One of our 7 ocean drones, we're directly hit by the lighting tsunami wave.

"What do you fellas think is causing this?"

"Atmospheric change."

In some places in India reported acidic rain, and hail storms with wind gusts up to 60 miles per hour. Flooding occurred in some of the streets.

These occurrences have been going on for a week, one of the drones is far out in the ocean and made a video of 2 twisters destroying a fishing vessel in the evening.

The fishing industry in the United States is valued at around 11.5 billion U.S. dollar, you certainly know your stuff.

The biggest fishing company is Trident Seafoods Corporation. Close to a third of all the world's fishing stocks are overfished, then we must put in place new policies and even make new laws if warranted said the president.

Recently the CEO of splendid seafood lost 10 crab vessels in the Bering Sea, 2 ocean drones caught on video the fate of the vessels. In the video we see, large waves slamming into the vessels.

Then bolts of blue lightning struck all around the ships, one of the crewmen jumped overboard and a minute later made a direct hit frying everything on the ships but they didn't sink.

An American towing ship with a Captain familiar with the Bering sea was sent out to find the crab ships, with the help of advanced radar it showed where the scattered ships were all around the Bering sea.

Then radioed back to base, and 5 more towing ships went out to tow the rest of the crab ships back to the docks.

Sadly the entire crews on the crab ships were killed, the owner of the company paid for the men to be buried.

The CEO has banned his fishing vessels from fishing in the Bering sea due to the odd lighting storms. I couldn't imagine working on a crab ship, those men endure so much.

> "Does every bolt of lighting have the same amount of electricity running through it?"
>
> "The currents aren't the same."
>
> "How long is a bolt of lightning?"
>
> "They're typically two to three miles long."

Ocean lightning storms are larger than land lightning storms, Lightning isn't evenly distributed across our planet.

Every year lightning causes billions of dollars in damage to our delicate vital electrical grid and many other communication devices.

Globally, there are 40 to 50 flashes of lightning that occur every second, that comes out to 1.4 billion flashes per year.

Among all the states in the United States, Florida has the highest frequency of lightning. The Great Galveston Hurricane of 1900 was the deadliest and the strongest hurricane to hit the United States, causing thousands of deaths. A million-dollar solar research drone that has been flying over the oceans monitoring ocean conditions was struck by a bolt of lightning.

> "Do you know how many research drones are in the world?"
>
> "No."

There are 1 million of them, and probably more being built as we speak. There are currently 11,000 defense drones that belong to the department of defense.

My concern is how many new drones that the Iranian military has, there naval power is rising. The US navy will put Irans navy in it's place.

The president adjusted his tie and peered out the window, this is the worst news I've heard in a week.

You gentlemen keep on telling me how bad the lightning storms are but you aren't giving me any ideas on how to stop it, I don't want to hear any theories either.

Just tell me how it's going to be solved, we need to stop the spraying chemtrails in the sky. My administration will not let me put an end to the spraying program.

I'm sure you think that I don't know anything about it, but I do. The first chemtrail spraying tests on U. S. cities were conducted in 1997.

All 50 States in the US, and every NATO country are now being sprayed every day. The spraying of biological and chemicals agents on U. S. Citizens is Illegal!.

The American people aren't even told when they'll be sprayed next, or why they're even being sprayed in the first place.

You must do something drastic to make this right, you just go about your business not caring about your people. We the people have had enough of these bureaucratic games.

Farmers are having there farms taken away from them, so that the elite can build whatever they want on them. The economy is tanking, your administration has permanently turned it's back on the American people.

If you try to sell my land to China there will be a problem because I'll shoot back. You go ahead and bring your IRS army to my doorstep, I'll make quick work of them. The president shook his head in digust, I don't know where in the world your hearing this stuff from. Were working on a new economy bill, it should lower inflation and lower gas prices. Then you say you're going to ban gas cars in a few years. We may not ban gas vehicles, until 2040. Your clean air anisitive isn't doing anything, it will soon.

Chapter 2

Now our country has no more oil reserves because you sent it to another country. That's not true, that's fake news.

We have millions of gallons of oil set away at camp David. That's just great, but that's not going to help us. Inflation is so bad just a loaf of bread costs me $25, and who can afford a container of coffee for almost $40 dollars.

While you're sitting on trillions, soon we'll be a quadtrillon in debt. While you make tax cuts for the rich. Were working on a stimulus package and were looking into new ways to lower our spending.

Were going to not fund anymore other countries next year. We heard that our country and other countries are using weather warfare against one another, I can't talk about that, not to the public.

You can continue now; tuna fish are washing up on the beaches by the hundreds. We took a tuna fish to our lab for studying and what we found caught us by surprise.

It's bodies levels of potassium was off the charts, and it's dorsal fin was missing and so were it's eyes.

"What do you think is causing that?"

"The water is heating up causing, which is causing a kind of bacteria that preys on the eyes of fish to grow."

"How much of the ocean has this bacteria taken over?"

"8%."

"How long will it take until it takes over the oceans?"

"Less than a year."

The president leaned back in his chair; all of the beaches have been cleared of fish. You haven't mentioned to me about the blue whale situation, I'm getting to that.

There's currently a rise in their population, but they're struggling to keep their young safe from the killer whales.

I’ve read that there's been an explosion in the shrimp population, the good news is the shrimps will feed on the bacteria. The president glanced down at his watch, then looked up at the men.

“Is there something wrong Mr. President?”

“No,” we're just running out of time.

We still have 45 minutes to chat, then I’ll have to go. He handed the president papers out of his notebook, outlined in the papers is the rest of the issues with the ocean.

I almost forgot to mention this, 10 of the 50 ocean windmills off the coast of Florida have been demolished by many large waves.

I’m sure that the engineers will find a way to make a wave barrier to stop the waves. 45 minutes later, they finished discussing issues with the ocean.

The president stood up and walked around the room to stretch his legs. The atmospheric scientists asked the president a question and left.

Immediately after they left the president got on the phone with NASA, hello who are we speaking with? The President. Hold on I'll transfer you over to Doug. After hearing some elevator music, he picked up.

Hello Mr. President, I need your expertise Sir. I'm sure you know about the ozone layer issues that we're having, I do. I want to know what you're planning to do to repair the ozone layer, I don't know if you know about the machine that we have.

I know very little about it, I'll teach you. We currently have 15 of these machines, two of them are currently on Mars. The machine is called the Truxin, it can create oxygen and ozone and make an atmosphere on other planets.

It took 2 years to create this machine, and four weeks to build 1. While the president was on the phone one of his aids walked in and put a post it note on his desk and quietly left the room.

I'll briefly explain to you how it works compressed air, enters the electrolysis unit where it's electrochemically split into oxygen and carbon monoxide.

"What's electrochemical?"

"Is the mode of energy that's used for deburring."

Together electrochemical chemical deburring refers to a machining process where burrs are taken out by using electrochemical energy.

"Can we put the 15 machines to work?"

"Sure, we can but one of them needs repair."

I want you to test each and every one of them after we hang up, I'll be sure to do that. Then I want you to fire them up tomorrow, because it's dire that we repair the ozone layer. Sounds good I'll talk to you later, bye now.

The president called the Oceanic research facility. A woman answered the phone with a chipper hello, hi I'm the president.

"What can we do for you today?"

"I need to be transferred to Vince."

After just three rings Vince picked up the phone, hello Sir it's been a while since we've talked.

"What is it you'd like to discuss with me?"

"What are you doing to repair the oceans?"

"We've been spraying chemicals over them to kill the bad bacteria, and it'll lower the fishes potassium level to the correct level."

Within two hours after we spray thousands of bacteria die off.

"How do you know where the bacteria is growing from up in the plane?"

"Because the bacteria makes the water turn yellow."

"How are the tsunami barriers holding up in California?"

"They have received minimal damage."

"How are we going to stop the lightning storms?"

"We'll spray Hemtrucus over the oceans overnight, that should calm the sky."

"What's Hemtrucus?"

"It's a combination of 3 chemicals."

I'm glad to hear that the oceans are being taken care of, I apologize Sir but I have to be somewhere now, no need to apologize I'll talk to you later bye.

Several months later the Atlantic Ocean dried up, and a part of the Pacific Ocean dried up. The ozone layer machines malfunctioned, and because of that the rest of the remaining delicate ozone layer collapsed.

Some kind of invisible particles had completely surrounded the Earth, the very next day tragedy struck when everyone accept a few scientists were left in the world.

They studied Cellular Biology at Carson University. The World leaders disappeared, just like everyone else did.

Hopeton is living in a laboratory in Antarctica, while his colleagues are all alone in different areas of the world.

Chapter 3

Lavonte is living somewhere in the wilderness of Alaska, he has built a small makeshift shelter for himself. To stay warm during the cold days and nights he has two campfires situated by his shelter.

Just two hours ago he was scrimmaging around for more wood, when he came upon a knocked over tent. He bent down to take a closer look in the tent, there was an old broken Lantern and a rifle.

He picked up the rifle and began looking it over. He took out the magazine and saw that it was fully loaded. In the brush nearby he could hear branches snapping, the birds that were on the branches nearby flew away.

He was sitting on a fallen tree and remained motionless, wondering what large creature was going to come out of the woods any moment. A grizzly bear came out of the woods, there was an arrow sticking out of its side.

It's one leg was covered in blood, it stood up on its hind legs and sniffed the air. Rather than shooting the bear, he walked back to his shelter. He figured that the campfires, would be enough to deter the bear.

A crow landed in a tree just a few feet away from him. The crow began to squawk, he picked up a small stick and threw it at the bird quieting it down. He was glad to see that the bear was no longer insight, the winds began to pick up.

He pulled his hoodie over his head and laid down by the fire. He had piles of wood around this campfires, he decided to head into his shelter and take a rest.

Nibaw was living in Iceland in the house that he had renovated a year ago, he's beginning to run out of food.

For his birthday last year his friend got him a packet of different seeds to plant, out of all the other plants the tomato plants grew the best.

He wasn't even sure if his asparagus plants are growing, while he was looking around for something in his cabinet, he stumbled upon meat in a mason jar. When he opened the mason jar, the putrid smell of it made him cough.

He immediately threw it in the trash can, then went on to check on his hydroponic system. He noticed that the lettuce was growing well, and the broccoli plants looked good as well.

There was a pesky fly flying around the room, he grabbed the flyswatter and as soon as it landed he hit it. He glanced out the window for a moment and turned his head when he saw that it was raining.

Sadly, though he lost his girlfriend several weeks ago, she went hiking somewhere and never made it back. He spent several days looking for her, but there were no sign of her.

His horses keep him from becoming lonely, Sunny and Dale are well behaved and like to swim.

He takes them in the lake, and they happily swim. He oftentimes thinks about the days when he used to work with Hopeton, but since the world ended and most of the population just disappeared he's become saddened. The other day he hot wired a car just to go take a short ride around the town.

During his days working alongside Hopeton, studying Oceanography and Marine biology they made one major discovery. Ogima is living in a one-bedroom apartment near an ocean research facility, that opened in 1996.

The research facility was destroyed after a tractor trailer crashed into it and didn't have the funds to get it fixed and they closed down. She is currently looking for water to drink, no more water came out of the faucet.

She hasn't come across a creek nearby yet and is becoming more concerned as time goes on. Before she left the apartment, she let her pet pigeons go loose and gathered up all of her belongings that she was going to take with her.

She had everything packed in her backpack and put it over her shoulders. She's been a marine biologist for 22 years now, her favorite animal is the dolphin.

A year and a half before everyone disappeared, she vacationed at a friend's beach house. Nearby to the beach house there was a dolphin rescue facility. During that time, they had 15 rescued dolphins, she would swim round in the lagoon.

The people at the facility were glad to see her swimming with the dolphins, she would swim around for at least an hour. Unfortunately, her friend couldn't enjoy dolphins with her because she couldn't swim.

Ogima said to her many times that she would teach her how to swim, but she always declined her. Even her friend had disappeared, this left her down for several days.

As she was walking down a country road, she could sense that something was following her. She quickly slipped her backpack off her shoulders, and opened one of the compartments and took out a pistol.

Then she put the backpack back on and kept on walking. Whatever it was, it was a lot closer to her now because she could hear it rustling through the leaves. Sometime later she walked past the grocery store that she used to go to, it was all rundown.

There were shopping carts scattered haphazardly in the parking lot. She turned around and a rabid fox came running out of nowhere, she immediately shot it. After that excursion she set up a makeshift shelter for the night.

The worlds infrastructure is seriously falling apart, several bridges in several different countries have collapsed.

In the United States an aging apartment building collapsed, crushing cars and everything else below it.

A hurricane passed through Louisiana and Georgia destroying houses, knocking down power lines and damaging vehicles.

The nuclear power plant in the largest city in the world malfunctioned and later that week exploded, turning everything in its path into dust.

Just about every building in the city was destroyed along with the wild life in the area. Everyone's pets in the world either escaped the homes they were in or starved to death.

In the Philadelphia Zoo there were several lions, some of the lions took their chances and smashed through a barrier and escaped.

They ran out into the open streets; some dogs began to bark at them. They chased after one of the dogs, the dog jumped over a car to escape the lion and bumped into a bear.

The bear stood up on its back legs and didn't chase after the dog. The dog ran to the end of the block and laid down, while the lions were fighting over the carcass of a dead cow.

A terrible windstorm fiercely tore through a street in Manhattan, overturning vehicles and tearing trees completely out of the ground.

Birds were blown out of the sky and flew into the buildings. The streets were partially flooded due to a water vein exploding a day ago. An electrical fire caused an office building to burn to the ground in two hours.

Chapter 4

The building beside it also caught fire and burned down. A massive earthquake shook Brooklyn, causing five buildings to collapse.

The foundation of the local firehouse was cracked, and two sink holes developed in front of a plaza.

Two cars fell into the second sink hole along with a telephone pole. In Detroit it rained for three days, and the streets were severely flooded, and it caused the power grid to short out.

In the Ukraine three storms flooded out the homes in its capital city, cars were floating down the street. A massive earthquake occurred beside the Eiffel Tower, causing it to topple over.

Twisted pieces of it laid everywhere in the rat-infested street. In Australia millions of mice took refuge in the abandoned homes, farms, and bars.

In Cuba, a huge storm that developed far out in the ocean, caused huge waves to slam into the island with tremendous force.

A huge chunk of a building collapsed into the street. Two buildings collapsed crushing two antique cars and a street sign.

The boats in the marinas capsized and the wood from one pier smashed into a speed boat causing it to leak fuel into the ocean.

A hailstorm developed over Cuba damaging everything in its path, this caused considerable damage to the capital building weakening the entire structure. The helicopter pad on top of the building cracked apart, causing the helicopter to plummet to the ground falling into several pieces. A military bunker underneath Kuwait collapsed due to not being maintained and because of a minor quake. The city of Kuwait was eaten up by an enormous sinkhole. Saudi Arabia suffered the most catastrophic incidents,

One of the sky scrappers fell down from a two hundred mile-per-hour dust storm, within forty-five minutes the building had fallen over the top of a hydroelectric plant causing it to explode into a fiery inferno.

The fire lasted for three hours destroying a convenience store and many other buildings including a gun powder manufacturing building. Ten thousand pounds of explosive went off.

The devastating magnitude 9.1 earthquakes that occurred off the west coast of Sumatra, Indonesia, was the Indian Ocean earthquake followed by a tsunami. An enormous tsunami was caused by the earthquake.

In South Asian and East African nations, destroying infrastructure. The earthquake and tsunami are thought to have caused billions in damages.

The Tacoma Narrows Bridge, which now serves as a classic case study in poor engineering, collapsed less than six months after it was inaugurated.

Due to the bridge's tendency to twist and buckle in even light winds, it was given the name "Galloping Gertie".

Its final collapse was ultimately brought on by the use of cheap and short plate girders and 40 mph winds.

Kemper Arena, was renowned for its inventive and flawless design, which even earned its architect a prize. The arena had a temporary reservoir and a flat top to lessen rainwater runoff.

When a storm dropped greater than four inches of rainfall on Kansas City, the roof fell because it couldn't withstand greater than two inches of rain without spilling.

Even though the arena was empty, portions of its walls were blown out by the catastrophic fall. Rafael Violy's curving glass structures, which he created in both London and Las Vegas, unintentionally served as a magnifying glass.

It was above "160 degrees Fahrenheit, notoriously melting a man's Jaguar, and growing so hot you could cook an egg on the pavement" as the sun's reflection heated the streets below.

In addition, the London structure produced a wind tunnel that was so powerful that it overturned carts, street signs. At the Hyatt Regency Hotel in Missouri, a raised walkway collapsed.

The walkway from the fourth story gave way and fell onto the walkway two floors below, smashing into the lounge.

Due to the manner in, which the walkways were fastened together one below the other, generating "immense and unnecessary stress," this structural breakdown happened during the design phase.

The Hard Rock Hotel fell down out of nowhere. Numerous victims reported dangerous building conditions and procedures. This occurred just a month before the end of the world.

Over 50 automobiles were lost in the Mississippi River after a bridge collapsed. Which had been made worse by workers pouring concrete and weakening a part of the bridge that was already crumbling. The test had been performed before, but this time there was a power surge, making it impossible for experts to turn off Chornobyl's nuclear reactors. In the early morning hours of April 26, 1986, the Chernobyl Nuclear Power Plant in Ukraine (formerly part of the Soviet Union) exploded.

One reactor had a steam buildup, roof collapse, nuclear core exposure, and radioactive material leakage into the atmosphere.

Studies predict that hundreds of individuals have died from cancer as a result of the radiation in the years since the tragedy. It's also one of the costliest disasters in recorded history.This caused damage to the ozone layer.

Asbestos was present in the vermiculite at Libby, Montana, and the mining firm was aware of its harmful consequences.

However, they kept it a secret, and residents of Libby used the mine's leftover materials for construction and landscaping, as well as for skating rinks and school projects.

As a consequence, roughly 10% of the town's residents passed away from an asbestos-related sickness, and those who perished weren't always miners because asbestos fibers are easily transmitted to other individuals. An exploratory oil well was being drilled by the Deepwater Horizon oil rig, a floating platform.

This in and of itself was not an issue, as the rig was working well within its capabilities. Later, however, methane gas from the undersea well erupted and spread inside the drilling equipment before igniting and detonating.

Eleven employees were killed in the explosion, which immediately destroyed the whole drilling platform.

Ninety-four crew members were also evacuated. The rig sank two days later. This only lessened peoples trust in drilling platforms. In Bhopal, India, a pesticide factory had a gas leak.

A runaway pressure rise caused by failing safety systems led to the release of 40 tonnes of the chemical methyl isocyanate into the atmosphere.

More than 600,000 individuals were exposed to the lethal cloud since there was such a significant volume of poisonous material there and the factory was bordered by a congested neighborhood.

Hundreds of innocent individuals died within hours as a result of coughing, eye irritation, burns, dyspnea, and vomiting. Additionally, thousands of animals died.

Chapter 5

Most people imagine lava streaming from a volcano, yet the largest mud volcano in the world is located in Sidoarjo, Indonesia. An explosion at a gas well that an energy firm had dug caused it to occur.

This Indonesian occurrence, where a borehole was dug, is likely the only one brought induced by human action.

This led neighboring ground to erupt with water, steam, and gas; the next day, water, steam, and mud started to surface once again; and they have continued to do so ever since. The volcano first released more than 6.3 million cubic feet of mud every day.

A pipeline explosion resulted in the deaths of eleven individuals, and 30,000 people had to be evacuated.

More than 10,000 houses and 12 towns were completely demolished, and metal from the mud flow polluted adjacent rivers.

There are more than just drink bottles and crisp packs in the Great Pacific Garbage Patch. Ecologists believe that 70% of ocean waste falls to the bottom of the sea, so there may be far more below the surface.

The majority of the plastic in the area has degraded into small bits that only give the water a foggy appearance.

Because plastic on the ocean's surface can prevent algae and plankton from receiving sunlight and because various types of plastics can leak toxins, the patch also has a significant and negative influence on the ecosystems and food chains of the ocean.

Wildfires are now a far more frequent hazard due to climate change. Climate change caused a rise in temperatures in the years before the fires, which destroyed a lot of Californian trees and provided enough fuel for flames to spread.

Observed many explosions at a petrochemical facility. About 110 tons of pollutants were spilled into the Songhua River as a result of the explosions.

Both in the Sea of Japan and Russian cities, chemicals have been found. This fire started during the show while a circus was in progress and quickly spread, putting the entire theater on fire.

This was the most devastating incident to ever affect the Lehman Theater in St. Petersburg, Russia. The catastrophe resulted in over 800 deaths. All this occurred 3 years before the world ended.

A 30-year-old male citizen of Lebanon and a 28-year-old Russian woman were prosecuted for drinking juice in public during Ramadan based on a court decision and had to pay a rather sizable fine. They were prosecuted in court for drinking juice.

A couple who were discovered on a beach and who were allegedly in the lifeguard shack in a compromising manner was given a year in prison and deported.

The fact that a man was arrested for having poppy seeds on his clothes from a bread roll he had at the same airport kind of sealed the deal even though we already knew Dubai had nearly unbelievable severe drug policies.

More than 70% of Haitians were living in poverty prior to the magnitude 7.0 earthquake due to political unrest and a failing economy, a cycle of instability that still exists today. There was poor infrastructure, and many people lived in shantytowns.

But the devastation of the earthquake was difficult to imagine. More than 220,000 individuals, or at least 2% of the population, died.

There were 1.5 million displaced people. A storm that was forecast suddenly became the biggest hurricane, wreaking massive destruction throughout the Caribbean.

For days, electricity and heat were cut off to people, and many of them were stuck in high-rise structures without any way to escape or get supplies.

In only the United States, over 100 people lost their lives, many from exposure or diseases associated with it.

The incident put many Americans' feeling of security in jeopardy, and the media frenzy around apparently unstoppable New York City - already one of the world's media hubs - was unparalleled.

One of the strongest hurricanes "super typhoon" struck the Philippines with winds of close to 200 mph. Haiyan was going to be terrible no matter what.

But it was difficult to comprehend the disaster's overwhelming size. The storm surge, which in some places exceeded 20 feet, stunned the whole globe.

It left destruction in its path as it raced through highly inhabited regions, including Tacloban, a significant metropolis.

Over 4 million people were left homeless and over 7,000 individuals died as a result of the storm.

The most lethal Ebola epidemic in history started in Guinea and rapidly moved to Sierra Leone and Liberia, primarily affecting metropolitan areas.

Over the course of two years, more than 11,000 individuals died from Ebola, accounting for around 40% of those who contracted the disease.

The speed and extent of the outbreak terrified everyone, and industrialized nations were worried about their security because Ebola cases had even spread to the United States and Europe.

The international community sprang in to support regional initiatives. Increased focus on vaccinations and treatments—some of which are currently being employed in the battle against the current epidemic in the Democratic Republic of the Congo—was also prompted by worries about the disease's impending doom. Despite the fact that the earthquake occurred on a Saturday afternoon when many people were outside of their homes.

Chapter 6

Nepal's fragile architecture made it particularly perilous. Due to Nepal's rugged geography, which made it challenging to access distant locations.

The terrible hurricane left destruction in its path when it first struck Dominica and then Puerto Rico. However, the storm brought Puerto Rico's position as a US territory to light in particular.

One of the most developed nations in the world's 3.4 million residents experienced months-long power outages.

The lack of electricity is also believed to have played a significant role in many of the 3,000 deaths linked to the storm. Additionally, government help has been late to arrive and still is, raising questions about unfair treatment.

In Indonesia and the Amazon, slash-and-burn agriculture sparked enormous, catastrophic wildfires that destroyed the region's precious forests and rainforest areas.

The fires put beef ranchers and producers of palm oil against the global community, bringing up the question of how to fulfill individual needs as the world strives to combat climate change and preserve precious landscapes. Months after the Camp Fire in California, which rocked the nation, a series of wildfires erupted throughout the state, raising concerns about the possibility of future, massive, climate-related flames.

One of the worst earthquakes to strike the Gulf Coast in recent years was Hurricane Katrina. Apparently, it was the sixth-strongest earthquake to ever strike the United States.

Both the number of individuals who died and the amount of damage were significant. In actuality, this hurricane caused about $81 billion in damages that needed to be fixed. It had disastrous repercussions.

After quite some time, the scientist and his colleagues were able to find one another then meet up.

Together they journeyed to the Atlantic Ocean, where they found some kind of mysterious machine. Hopeton saw that it said water machine, he couldn't believe his luck.

> “Are you going to start that thing up professor?”
>
> “I'm going to try to.”
>
> “Would you like some help with that?”
>
> “No,” thanks I can get it.

He pushed in a switch, that said on. He saw a button that red two days, five days, or eight days. One of his colleagues glanced over at it.

"In an excited voice he asked how days are you going to put it on for?"

"5 days."

They left the area, and when they returned there was a pool of water. On the days to follow, they explored the world.

The End

www.ingramcontent.com/pod-product-compliance
Lightning Source LLC
LaVergne TN
LVHW052112160826
845678LV00015B/3508

9798352189344